Sparrowlegs

Paul Delaney

Published in 2015 by FeedARead.com Publishing

A CIP catalogue record for this title is available from the British Library.

'Spare, moving writing and a thrilling story!'

Michael Morpurgo

'This is one of the best stories I've ever read. It is full of imagination, pathos and human emotion. The author uses beautiful language to create a wonderful world for the reader.

(Pat Nolan – writer)

Paul Delaney is a poet, a writer, a teacher and a professional musician. He's also a dad to three seriously cool boys, Harry, George and Freddie. They are all super sporty but their dad wasn't. He packed in rugby once because somebody pushed him over and guess what?

They didn't even have the decency to say

sorry!

So Paul decided to learn how to play the piano, organ and write stories and poems instead. It's warm when you do these things too, as you're indoors and not outside standing in the wind and rain on a big field.

Also, you don't get cold and muddy but best of all is this:

NOBODY ever pushes you over!

This book is dedicated to the thousands of football (and rugby) coaches up and down the country, who week in, week out, deliver high quality coaching and organise competitive matches for our children for no financial reward. I salute your dedication to your sport, your teams and above all, to our children.

And to a lovely gentleman called Harold, whom I met at 'Finch Farm', Everton F.C.'s training ground on Sunday 27th October 2013. Thank you for all your help!

www.pdelaney.co.uk

'What a lovely day for a game of football.
All we need is some green grass and a ball...'

Bill Shankly
(Legendary Liverpool FC manager)

One

A few years ago, I lived in an old, terraced house. School was just down the road and the Bongs, as we called them, just a few streets away.

The 'Bongs' by the way, was a huge open field, with hilly bumps, scattered trees and a little pond. Dogs pulled their owners across the long, wet grass. Children flew their colourful kites in the strong winds. Footballers battled it out on the muddy pitch, chasing the ball across the puddles.

Every evening you'd find me down there. At weekends, it was the place to be. I'd play out in all weathers, with my best friends, Matty and Gadge.

They were twins but you couldn't tell. Crowning Matty's tall, slim body was a thick head of wavy brown hair. But Gadge was different. A short, cropped haircut sat on his head, like a thousand sharp straws.

We all went to the same school, sitting in Mr McDermott's cold, draughty classroom. We lived next door to each other too. I suppose you could say we were like brothers. We didn't look like it through.

I was probably the smallest boy on the playground in those days. The only one with red, curly hair and a hundred freckles covering my face like a volcanic rash. 'We're all different!' McDermott used to say. '

True Sir, I thought.

Matty and Gadge's skills with the football were incredible. But I wasn't so lucky. It was even written in black and white. 'Malcolm Thomas: tries really hard at football but only scores one goal every year – normally when the goalkeeper's tied up!'

That's what my teacher, Mr Ryan scribbled on my report one year. Mum's still got that crumpled up piece of paper somewhere. It still makes me chuckle when I read it. He was only joking about the goalkeeper of course but it did hurt a little.

I'll prove you wrong one day, Sir, I remember thinking as he breezed past me in the cold corridor. *And that's a promise.*

Matty, Gadge and I played for Stanley Village football club, the 'under elevens' team. Looking back, I think I was a little jealous of the twins. Everything was going right for them. Living with their parents, they seemed to have things I could only dream about.

How that sleek Mercedes saloon of theirs floated down the street! It was like a silent, black beast, its engine purring obediently. And the bodywork! No marks, no scratches and definitely no dints. It was pure, shining steel, like soft, polished moonlight, rolling down the road.

For holidays, Matty and Gadge would fly to the other side of the world on jumbo jets. Sometimes to places with strange names that I couldn't even say properly.

I'd be happy in Uncle Ron's car, travelling to Wales with Mum for a whole week in his caravan. Sometimes, we'd jump on a coach for a day out to Blackpool. 'First one to see the tower wins a pound!' Mum would say.

I fell in love with the twins' panther black 'Goal hunger' football boots. They were black leather, with a thin, golden stripe running down the sides. Six silver studs screwed into the tough, plastic soles. Long, silver laces hung from those boots like strands of angels' hair.

How often had I stared at those magical boots, lying in the dusty display window of Boydells, our local sports shop? My eyes widened in wonder, locked onto this heavenly image. I stared at them for an age, my fingertips digging into the shop's cold glass.

'I'm not made of money, love,' Mum said softly, dragging a mouthful of cigarette smoke into her lungs. 'Well unless I win at the bingo this weekend and if that happens, I'll buy you two pairs!'

So I pulled the 'Boots with no name' onto my feet. It was the moulded, plastic studs I hated the most. Not 'screw-ins' but already stuck to the bottom of the black, rubbery soles.

I didn't like those boots one little bit. They were too tight anyway, squashing my toes together. They turned my feet into two tight, clenched fists, almost bursting out of their leathery prison.

Football training was hard work. We were always out after school, even when snow clouds drifted across the sky. Nothing would stop us getting out onto the field, not even a sudden earthquake.

We trained with the school team on the big field and we trained with Stanley F.C. on the Bongs. And do you know what? We loved every minute of it, lapping it all up like a pack of hungry hounds gnawing on a bag of butcher's bones.

Everybody had somebody watching them. Except me. Mum tried to get to training as much as she could. She showed her face at a rare weekend match. But most of the time she was stuck behind the counter in Graham's busy bakery.

'You do understand, don't you?' she whispered in that soft voice of hers, her eyes deep and searching. 'It's just a little overtime and I'll put the extra money in the holiday pot!'

But the holiday pot, an old jam jar, was almost always empty. Mum would hand those spare coins and notes over the counter in Reeves' dusty corner shop. And Mr Reeves would exchange them for cigarettes, whiskey and a small bottle of lemonade.

A little hurt often came my way during training, like a short, sharp unexpected pinch. 'Substitute – Malcolm Thomas' the team sheet would read, scribbled out in ballpoint pen. *You'll get into the team one day,* I'd say to myself, watching the game unfold. *If aliens land and kidnap most of the team.*

Looking back, I wasn't a bad footballer. I had a few skills up my sleeve. Passing the ball in a smooth, straight line, I'd find the feet of another player almost every time. I could shoot with both feet too, sometime driving the ball into the back of the net. I think it was my self-confidence, that's all. I just didn't believe in myself at all. Not one little bit.

Hanging around with Matty and Gadge was great. 'Come on Malcolm!' they shouted out before training. 'Show your skills off!' They never laughed at me, even if I made a mistake. They just encouraged me, jumping high onto my shoulders when anybody scored. Now that made me feel good, that's for sure!

We played for hours in each other's bedrooms. We watched exciting games down at the local football ground too, cheering on Stanley's first team. We sneaked into the cinema to catch a glimpse of the latest films, all freshly delivered from Hollywood. We even went on days out together, in that luxury, floating machine of theirs.

I thought it would never end. Those days would last forever. But then, one cold, foggy morning, on 6th November 1999, it finally happened.

A large, blue transit van screeched to a sudden halt outside Number 25 Badger Street. Two scruffy workers jumped out into Matty and Gadge's front garden. One of them held a tall, thin wooden pole with a rectangular sign at the top. The other one hammered it into the soft ground. 'House for sale' the sign said, in thick, black letters.

Two

It all seemed to happen so quickly. One minute the sign was up. The next minute the house was empty. 'Dad's got a new job in London,' Matty beamed, bouncing his leather football. 'I can't wait to see Wembley!'

We said we'd keep in touch but we never did. After several weeks of writing to each other, our letters dried up. To this day I don't really know why. 'When you've gone, you've gone,' Mum used to say.

I suppose things naturally move on don't they? For weeks, I sobbed into my damp pillow. I wanted my special friends to come back. I wanted to see their faces and hear their voices. I dreamed and waited. I waited and dreamed. But alas, it was no good.

I played on my own in the street, hoping to catch a glimpse of the floating black beast.

My mind filled up with whispering voices. *We're coming home Malcolm! Mum didn't like London at all, said it was too noisy!*

But finally, it hit me, like a sledgehammer splitting a stone. My best friends were gone - forever.

My bones ached with excitement when Mum dashed into my bedroom one cold, January evening. 'Joan told me in the shop,' she exclaimed. 'A new family's moving in soon. And guess what? They've got three young boys, all about your age...and they're all football crazy!'

Staring out of my bedroom window, I waited for weeks. My head spun thousands of times. The slightest noise and I'd be off my bed, my nose pressed up against the cold, frosty glass.

A car pulling up outside perhaps. The loud piercing horn of a taxicab. The sharp screech of the Number 47's brakes, dropping off old MrsProsser as usual. Or the faint whirr of Geoff's milk float, creeping up the street along with dozens of empty, rattling bottles. But nothing happened. Nothing at all.

Until that cold, February morning. A thin cloak of fog was lifting when I saw him for the first time. Standing in my front garden, my hands trembled with sharp, painful cold.

He was in a silver wheelchair, with a thick, red blanket draped over his knees. Somebody was pushing him up the path of 'Shell Green' cottage. I held my breath. Tears invaded the whites of my eyes. I tore up my welcome card I'd made for the Harvey boys.

Slumped in that rickety old chair, an old aged pensioner sat. On the top of his bald head, a few tangled hairs blew in the wind like grey, dancing spiders. He was covered in long, thin wrinkles, etched into his face like deep scars. He was half asleep. Half dead I suppose.

Peering at him, I shook my head. My mouth closed as my eyes narrowed. A long, unhappy sigh escaped through my lips. I released a sad, cloudy breath into the cold air.

The lady pushing him pulled a key from her pocket. Then she put it into the lock, pushing the wide, black door open.

Struggling to lift the wheelchair over a huge, whitewashed stone step, she paused. For several seconds, they both chatted away. Two icy breaths locked together, rising up into the freezing heavens.

Then she grappled with his frail, lame body. She pulled him up from his wheelchair prison. Slowly, the old man rose to his unsteady feet.

Her loving arms around his shoulders, they strode over the tall step into the warmth of the house. The hairs on my back rose up. I found myself out of breath. Perhaps I was scared of his wheelchair, I thought.

'This is the worst day of my life!' I screamed to Mum. A thick cloud of sadness suffocated my heart, almost strangling its heavy beats. 'I've no new friends to play with now, just an old man who probably can't even play cards.'

'Don't be so heartless, Malcolm,' Mum said. Her eyes smoked with anger, almost drilling through my forehead.

'But he's in a wheelchair, Mum!' I snapped. 'I've seen it with my own eyes. He can't even walk. He can't do anything, except breathe probably.'

Mum gazed at me. She ran her bony fingers through her thick, brown hair, tinged with little flecks of grey. 'You might be in a wheelchair yourself one day, Malcolm!' she bawled. 'I can't believe you're being so horrible!'

'It's just that the Harvey boys…'

'Their parents didn't like the house,' Mum interrupted. 'Thought the kitchen was too small or something. Wanted a garden instead of a back yard. That's what I heard anyway.'

'Well it stinks!' I barked. 'I've got nobody to play football with again, have I? Why can't we move down to London? Or haven't we got any money *as usual*?'

I think I said the wrong thing. A horrible, ghoulish scream erupted from Mum's mouth at dangerous speed. She dashed towards me. I avoided her angry clutches by running into the hall and leaping upstairs two steps at a time.

'Don't you dare show your face down here!' she yelled. 'You ungrateful little brat!'

Lying on my bedroom carpet, I stared at the ceiling. I clamped both eyes shut. Thoughts raced through my battered head like hot, electric sparks dancing off a welder's torch.

I saw the wheelchair. I was the old man, his head bowed in defeat. I saw his helper, struggling to pull this thin bag of bones over the step. Then I saw Mum, slaving away behind Graham's busy counter. Just for a few extra pounds in her purse.

The sound of Mum's quiet sobbing crept under my bedroom door. Pulling it ajar, I snuck out onto the landing. Soon, I was sitting on a step halfway down the stairs.

Watching her through the kitchen doorway, she sat tall on a wooden stool. A smoky cigarette was balanced between two shaking fingers. A tall glass of whiskey hung from her other hand too. Her whole body seemed to be trembling.

'Sorry Mum,' I whispered as I sidled up to her. I lowered my head, eyes glued to the clay floor tiles. 'It's just that…'

'One day Malcolm, you'll realise just how tough it's been,' she said.

She sucked on the end of her cigarette, its stale smoke rising into the air. Staring at me, she drilled deep holes right through the centres of my eyes. 'I hate working all day and leaving you. But what else can I do?'

'I know Mum,' I sheepishly replied, watching the curling, twisting smoke trails.

'It's hard enough being on my own all the time,' Mum added. 'I get lonely too, you know. But at least you could be grateful Malcolm. Money doesn't grow on trees.'

'I'm sorry, Mum,' I whispered, burying my head into her warm lap. 'And I'll always love you, you know that don't you?'

'I love you too, Malcolm,' she said. 'So that's why I want you to respect the man in the wheelchair. He's a human being, just like you and me. And he was a young man once, so just remember that!'

Wiping away her tears with a small, soft tissue, she looked straight through me. 'Anyway, his name's Mr Schiaffino,' she said, as a tiny smile cracked open on her lips. 'He lives on his own but somebody looks after him. So guess where we're going tonight?'

Open-mouthed, I twisted my head around, almost pulling a muscle. I stared into her for a few tense seconds, pulling away a little.

'But I don't want to go, Mum,' I said. 'It's just that, well; I don't like old people at all. You know that anyway.'

'Why not?'

'Because I don't, that's why!'

'Well we're going and that's the end of it,' Mum snapped, pouring the last drops of alcohol into her mouth. 'Anyway, don't be so selfish Malcolm. You'll be old yourself one day and believe me, it comes around sooner than you think.'

'But I don't want to go, Mum,' I said, puffing out a long, whining breath. Once more, I lowered my head, hiding my tear filled eyes. 'You can't force me!'

'Just do this for me Malcolm, please,' Mum said. 'Just for me, eh?'

Three

Mum knocked on the door. It opened with a gentle creak. A tall, thin lady was standing in the doorway, her bright yellow dress almost blinding us. A long mane of thick, black hair tumbled down her back.

'Uncle Joe's expecting you,' she said, her voice crackling with excitement. 'Oh, I'm Charlotte by the way, Joe's niece. Very pleased to meet you!'

Living a few streets away, she dropped in on her uncle every single day. 'Auntie Maria died a couple of years ago now,' Charlotte said, leading us down a dark, narrow hallway. 'And Uncle Joe's never been the same really. He thinks he can look after himself but he can't. Well not any more.'

'How old's your uncle?' Mum asked.

'Seventy five,' she whispered. 'And he's got the football on as usual. I can hear it.'

My eyes lit up like two locomotive lamps in a dark, smoky tunnel. Pushing open a door, Charlotte led us into a warm, cosy lounge. 'Uncle Joe, it's your new neighbours,' she said. 'Mrs Thomas and her son, err…'

'Malcolm,' I said as the cheers of excited football crowds weaved into my ears. Charlotte went off to make a pot of tea. Mum sat down on a small, leather sofa. I sat next to her, staring at Mr Schiaffino's bent over body.

Sitting in a tall, wooden armchair, a living skeleton glanced up at us. An enormous knitted cardigan hung from his shoulders like a grey, baggy ship's sail. His long, bony hands trembled a little.

Carved into his face, deep wrinkles stretched wide. A large pair of black spectacles rested upon his short, fat nose. And his dark, sunken eyes peered through thick lenses, like magnifying glasses.

'Corner ball!' he yelled in a strange accent. ''Bout time we had a bit of luck.'

He couldn't peel his eyes away from the football game. Mum asked him a few questions, but he just wasn't listening.

'Once the football starts, that's it,' Charlotte said as she trotted in with four mugs of tea. 'You might as well talk to the wall.'

'Do you like football?' Mr Schiaffino said, scratching his flaking, blotchy scalp.

'I love it,' I replied.

Sipping his warm tea, he glanced over to me. 'Can stay if you want,' he said. 'Watch the match with me.'

I looked towards Mum. She shook her head. 'It's almost time for Malcolm's tea Mr Schiaffino,' she said. 'And he's got his homework to do, haven't you love?'

Shaking his head, Mr Schiaffno stared at us. 'Football's better than homework, isn't it Malcolm?' he chuckled. A wrinkly smile stretched across his rough face. 'And call me Joe from now on. It's Juan really but all my friends call me Joe. Well, those who are left of course.'

Pausing, his dry, cracked lips stretched into a wide smile. He ran his fingers over those few remaining grey hairs of his, flattening them a little. 'At one time, they used to call me Sparrowlegs,' he said. 'But that's another story Malcolm.'

The shot was fast, unexpected and clean. Into the top corner the ball flew. 'Like a rocket!' screamed the commentator's bubbling, high-pitched voice. 'What a superb goal!'

Springing up, Joe's head almost burst through the ceiling. His half-filled mug of tea crashed to the floor as he bounced back down onto a big, springy cushion.

'We deserved that!' he yelled, flashing three yellow, stained teeth. 'Come on lads!'

Widening my eyes, I locked a puzzled gaze onto Joe's worn face. Joe had suddenly come to life. He was as happy as a child clutching a bag of sweets. That sudden goal had breathed life into his frail body.

'Any good at football are you?' he asked, puffing out a long breath.

'Err not really.'

'Play for any teams?'

'Yes but only substitute normally.'

'Everybody starts somewhere.'

'I suppose so,' I said, nodding.

'Anyway, where do you play?'

'On the Bongs, Saturday mornings usually.'

'Well I'll be there on Saturday then,' Joe said, his lips stretching into a cheeky grin.

Four

Saturday morning soon arrived. 'Enjoy your training!' Mum said before slamming the front door. 'I'll bring a pie back for tea.'

Turning over in my bed, I looked at my alarm clock, happily ticking away. Time to get up. Weekend training always started early. But this morning, I couldn't crawl out of the covers.

Wrapped in my thick sheets like a warm, Egyptian mummy, I stared at the ceiling. I closed my eyes. Joe's ancient face drifted across my mind. I saw him sitting in his wheelchair, bouncing around on heavy, grey clouds.

'Do you like football?' I heard him shout, peering at me with red, volcanic eyes. 'No I don't!' I screamed. 'And I don't like you either old man.'

I jumped out of bed, punching my mattress with two hard fists. 'So I'm not going to football this morning. And it's all because of you!'

Later, I gobbled up a small bowl of cereal. I slipped on my jeans and t-shirt and put on my thick coat, pulling the hood over my head. Within a few minutes, I was on the Bongs. I perched on a tiny hillock in the distance, munching away on a few stale biscuits.

My heart turned heavy as I watched Stanley F.C. go through their paces. I wasn't the world's worst footballer but I did wonder why I bothered.

I enjoyed football and had some great friends in the team. But most of them lived many streets away. Some went to a different school anyway.

I suppose I didn't want Joe to come and watch me. I was scared of him. I was terrified of that wheelchair of his, for some reason. I definitely didn't want an old aged pensioner as a friend, thank you very much.

Nervously, I scanned the scene below, searching for his silver chariot. From the side-lines, a small crowd clapped and cheered in the sharp, morning chill. My eyes cut through the cold air but I couldn't see Joe anywhere.

Ahh well, that's good, I thought. *He's forgotten all about me. Typical, isn't it? Don't make a promise if you're going to break it, thanks. But I don't want to see you either. You're too old, you can't walk, you smell a bit and...*

'What are you doing Malcolm?' a gruff voice called out. I turned around. Sitting in that chair of his like a King on his throne, Joe's sharp gaze pierced my skin.

'Uncle Joe got up early especially to see you Malcolm, didn't you?' Charlotte said.

'Yes I did,' Joe said. 'And I even missed my porridge.'

An enormous breath of icy wind almost toppled us over. A few cold, lonely raindrops fell from the heavens, gently caressing my face. 'Err, err, it's too cold to play,' I stammered.

'But not too cold for the others, eh?' Joe remarked.

'I don't feel well actually!' I barked. 'And anyway, what's it got to do with you? Are you my dad or something?'

'Keep your hair on!' Joe said. 'I'm just making a point, that's all.'

'Well keep your thoughts to yourself then!' I snapped, my jaws crashing together like a crocodile's.

I couldn't stay any longer. Tears flooded into my eyes. 'Now do me a favour old man,' I roared. 'Leave me alone and go and poke your nose into somebody else's business!'

I turned and sprinted down the hill. Angrily, I kicked a hundred Dandelion heads off as they swayed in the strong winds.

'How was your training love?' Mum asked later on as we both popped chunks of beef into our mouths.

'Great,' I said.

'Did Joe come to watch you then?'

'Err, yes.'

'Are you sure?'

'Yes.'

'Positive?'

'I've told you, haven't I?' I snapped. 'Yes, he came to see me!'

I could tell by Mum's sullen, hypnotic face. She didn't even say one word. She didn't have to, either. She just carried on eating her chunks and I carried on eating mine. Staring into cold, silent space, we both munched away.

And at the same time, we both wondered.

Five

A few days later, I dashed home from school. I climbed up my path, treading on wilting weeds with the thick, dirty soles of my shoes. There he was, outside his front door, sitting in that wheelchair of his.

'Malcolm!' he shouted, waving an arm through the thick, cold air.

Dropping my head, I pretended I couldn't see him. I slipped my key from my pocket. I thrust it into the lock, disappearing inside.

About five minutes later, a heavy knock echoed through the house. Pulling open the door, I stood still, staring. A huge, wrinkly smile greeted me.

'You can't get rid of me that easily, you know,' the old man said, pulling up his red, woolly blanket. 'Can I come in then?' he asked. 'It's freezing out here.'

Linking her uncle's arm, Charlotte pulled him up. She helped him out of his wheelchair, pushing him over the step. He struggled to walk down my hall, stopping for breath every few steps. Soon, he was sitting in an armchair opposite me, holding a freshly made mug of tea.

'Your mum's told me a few things about you, Malcolm,' Joe said. Electric sparks seemed to light up his tired, worn eyes as he spoke.

'She said you're going off football, said you don't like it anymore.'

'It's just that my best friends left town, that's all,' I replied.

'Matty and Gadge you mean?'

'How do you know that?'

'I found their names scribbled on the walls behind some old wallpaper,' he said.

A wry smile appeared on his face. 'I'm into football myself,' he said. 'It's about the only thing that keeps me going. Football, cups of tea and the odd bar of chocolate!'

A hearty laugh, mixed with a thick, chesty cough escaped from his mouth. 'I played a lot when I was younger,' he said. 'Won a lot of medals too!'

Slightly shaking, Joe's arm pulled his hot tea to his mouth. 'The drink of the Gods!' he exclaimed, before taking a sip. 'Tastes a lot better with a biscuit though!'

I reached for a packet of chocolate digestives. Spreading them out onto a small china plate, I shook my head. My mouth formed a wide, happy smile.

'These are Mum's favourites,' I said, passing over the plate. 'So don't eat them all!'

'I've got to watch my weight Malcolm,' Joe chuckled. 'Or I'll never get a girlfriend!'

I joined him as we both laughed out loud.

Clasping his bony hand around three biscuits, Joe drew one of them to his dry lips. 'No, I only loved my Maria,' he said. 'And when she died, she took a part of me with her, I think. Anyway, I'm too old for all that kissing lark!'

Laughing once more, I stared at Joe as two digestives vanished into his mouth. Bits of biscuit cascaded down his grey cardigan like a long, crumbly fountain. He munched away, taking little sips of his tea in between.

'Well I'll be on the Bongs this Saturday morning,' he said, brushing down his cardigan. 'And if you're not there this time, I'll tell your mum that you ate all the biscuits and you wouldn't share them with me!'

A huge, cheeky smile rose to his lips as his eyes widened. 'Is it a deal?' he asked, holding out a crumby hand. 'It's a deal,' I smirked, shaking it heartily.

Six

'You're rubbish, Malcolm,' jeered Tony Smith, flicking the ball up into the air. 'Try playing chess, it's a lot easier.'

I took no notice. I tried to snatch the ball out of the air but lost my balance and fell over. I tried to curl the ball into the top corner of the goal. A good strike it was but the ball just plunged into the side netting.

'Penalty practice next!' our coach, Barry yelled, dashing past me. 'Come on Malcolm; show me what you're made of Son!'

Every time I tried to drive the ball into the big, open goalmouth, something strange happened. The ball was wide. Or it flew over the crossbar. Or it hit the post. Almost in, I thought.

'Sure you don't need glasses, Malcolm?' Tony snarled, bouncing the ball up and down.

I stared hard at the small, shivering crowd of parents. Huddled in the cold, they stood in little groups around the pitch, cheering and chatting away. Mum was slaving away in the shop as usual.

But where was Dad? Well Dad died when I was only nine years old. 'Keep smiling Son,' he'd said, just before he floated up to heaven. 'And remember, I'll always be watching you.'

He was a superb footballer, my dad. Almost every weekend he'd take me somewhere for a kick around. We spent hours on the Bongs, in the park, or on Bleak Hill. Wherever there was a patch of grass!

One day, Dad had to go into hospital. That's all I can remember about it. I was too little to understand at the time. Catching the bus, I'd travel with Mum through winding, leafy lanes to Dad's ward. Every day we did that for weeks and weeks.

Towards the end, Dad was almost always asleep. I'll never forget those last words he muttered to me just before he died. He didn't even lift his head up. His white, veiny eyes stared out at us like two clear glass marbles.

'I love you so much, Malcolm,' Dad whispered, pressing into my hand with his weakening fingers. 'But please promise me something, Son. Look after your mummy and always be happy and grateful.'

I looked into Dad's fading eyes, his spirit preparing for its heavenly flight. 'And you remember this, Malcolm,' he continued. 'I'll always be with you, watching you, helping you and protecting you but most of all loving you...'

Dad's fingers released their grip. His wispy breathing stopped. He was gone. I peered at Dad's empty body. Mum stared into me. I stared into Dad. And we both hugged into the warmth of each other and cried and cried.

Mum told me Dad would change into a Robin when he was watching us. 'Daddy told me himself, love,' she explained. 'A few days before he died.'

We even set up a bird table in the back garden but we only attracted the odd, hungry sparrow.

I stood still in the middle of the football pitch. Tears, like heavy, silver ball bearings, rolled softly down my cheeks.

I was back at Dad's hospital bedside. I wanted to hold him, feel him. Gently stroke his skin perhaps. Feel the sharp stubble on his chin rubbing up against my face when we wrestled on the carpet. But of course, it was impossible.

'Earth calling Malcolm!' Barry bawled, sprinting past me. 'What planet are you on Son? Come on!'

He hadn't noticed my thick cloak of sadness, covering my body like a mean, miserable mist. Neither had anybody else, to be fair.

Chasing the ball across the bumpy turf, I ran off, holding Dad's memory in the secret depths of my heart. I suppose that's why I didn't like old people.

I mean, my dad was only thirty-five when he died. So a deep anger was locked up inside me, bursting to escape. It just didn't make any sense to me at all.

Joe seemed alright though. Scanning the crowd, I looked for him. He wasn't there. There was no wheelchair in sight. The old man's probably forgotten all about me, I thought, chasing after the football once more.

Seven

Tony Smith was Stanley F.C.'s top goal-scorer. He wore the Captain's armband too. He was tall and strong, with a huge mass of wavy blonde hair.

Magically, his boots seemed to attract footballs like magnets pulling in paper clips. He'd shoot from anywhere. And the ball would fly into the back of the net like a hot cannon ball.

Goalkeepers, however tall, had no chance. Most of them never realised what had hit them. Until they were fishing the ball out of the back of the net, wondering what on earth had happened.

I'd see Tony's face in my dreams quite a lot. I'd be him in some of them too, scoring hundreds of goals. Then I'd wake up and it'd be me again, trying my best. But my best never seemed to be good enough. I wasn't a bad player. But I wanted to be the best.

'Switch on, Malcolm!' Barry yelled, pushing back his black greasy hair. 'Cup match in half and hour - win this one and we're in the final!'

Glancing at everybody, he scribbled down names into his grubby little notebook. Then he looked at me with those hard, narrow eyes of his.

'You don't mind if you don't play today, do you Malcolm?' he said. 'It's just that I need to try out a few new players.'

What he really meant to say was I could play, as long as an asteroid suddenly crashed into the pitch, squashing most of the team flat.

'Err, no problem, Barry,' I replied, holding back two little tears. My lip quivered but somehow, I held myself together. I wasn't playing today but a warm glow rushed through my bones.

A strong, fiery heat invaded my body. I knew then that I'd prove them all wrong one day. I just had to be patient. I had to practise my skills a little more, that's all.

'When's the match starting?' a familiar, husky voice shouted out. I turned around.

Peering at the thin, bunched up crowd, I saw him. Joe was sitting in his wheelchair, clutching his beloved red blanket. Charlotte had pushed him over the footpath to watch me.

'I thought you'd forgotten all about me,' I said.

'I know what you thought,' he replied. 'I couldn't find me flat cap, could I?'

'Are you playing today Malcolm?' Charlotte asked. 'No,' I said. 'Looks like I've been dropped.'

'Well Uncle Joe's been watching you, haven't you?'

'I have that,' Joe said, raising his grey, bushy eyebrows. A long, airy breath whistled from his mouth as he raised his old eyes high.

'I know what you're thinking,' I said; gazing at the long, damp grass. 'What's that?' he asked.

'You could play better yourself!'

'Oh no, not at my age, Malcolm,' he said, shaking his head. 'I did once but not anymore. Anyway, you could be really good. I've been watching you.'

'Have you got a magic wand under your blanket?' I said. ''Cause you'll probably need it you know.'

'All you need is a bit of coaching,' Joe said.

'Do you know anybody?' I asked.

'You're looking at him!' Joe chuckled, arching his lips into a wry, cheeky smile.

Eight

As luck would have it, spring was gently pushing winter aside. Light evenings, still with a sharp chill in the air, had just arrived.

So we'd be out on the Bongs most evenings. Joe's back yard was handy too, especially if the field was wet and muddy. But Joe worked me very hard. All my muscles filled with aches and pains as he put me through my paces.

'See that big white spot on the wall?' he said. 'Hit it five times on the run and I'll give you a pound towards those football boots you like.'

It seemed impossible at first, even hitting the target once. Sometimes, I'd be up to three or four hits on the run. And then I'd miss and Joe would make me start all over again. 'Oh

I've had enough of all this nonsense!' I scowled one evening. 'I'm going out to play.'

Without thinking, I stormed out of Joe's back yard. He didn't even shout anything at me. He just let me go, without uttering a single word.

I sprinted to the Bongs, crushing an innocent snail as I ran. Then I had a knock about with a few friends. But Joe's kind face was tumbling around in my mind. I couldn't get rid of him.

Feeling sorry for myself, I was soon dashing down the lanes again, on my way back home. Joe hadn't even moved. He was just sitting there, his bony hands clasped around a steaming mug of tea.

'I knew you'd come back, Malcolm,' he announced, releasing a long, wispy breath.

'I'm sorry, Joe,' I mumbled, cracking my fingers.

'If you want something, you've got to work for it Malcolm. It's important!'

'I know but…'

'There are NO shortcuts to success!' Joe interrupted, sitting bolt upright. 'That's what I was told when I was a player.'

'I know, Joe,' I said. 'But hitting that spot so many times; it's really difficult.'

'So's getting into the team,' he exclaimed. 'So come on. If you want something, you have to work for it.'

'You've said that already!' I snapped.

'I know!' Joe answered, raising his eyebrows. 'I just enjoy winding you up, that's all!'

I couldn't believe it when I finally hit the spot five times on the run. Joe cheered so much that his wheelchair almost toppled over. A huge, cheesy grin was plastered all over his face for days. Even a big bar of soap couldn't remove it.'

Mum couldn't believe it either. 'Practice makes perfect,' she said. 'Well done love, I'm proud of you!'

Joe wasn't always in his wheelchair. In the house, he'd struggle around on two old, wooden walking sticks. Sometimes, he'd balance on a wall, stopping for breath. But he was always happy and cheerful. This great big smile shone out of his heart like an everlasting, golden sunshine.

'What's the point in moaning?' he'd say. 'Doesn't get you anywhere, does it?'

Sometimes, I'd push him over to the Bongs myself. 'Watch the bumps!' he'd shout out as I raced down the uneven, stony path. 'It's like a flaming roller-coaster!'

Resting upon his lap was our snack bag. It was filled with thick sandwiches, a few chocolate biscuits and a bottle of watery orange squash. Normally, Charlotte prepared it but Mum did her bit too. She'd often drop two meat and potato pies into the bag, courtesy of Graham's shop.

All the time, Joe watched me with those fierce old eyes of his. He'd suddenly come alive, ranting and raving like some old army sergeant from the war. 'If you want something, Malcolm...'

'You've got to work for it!' I'd shout back, struggling to catch my breath.

'Anyway, put down the ball, dribble through the cones and then hit your target.'

I always did as I was told. I trusted him, you see. I dashed around on the Bongs with a thousand powerful batteries stuffed down my socks. Well it seemed like that, anyway!

I couldn't believe he was doing all this for me. So I was desperate to impress him.

'Corner practice,' he shouted out on the field. 'Float the ball high up into the air. Visualise the position of your attackers!'

'Heading practice,' he shouted. 'I'll throw the ball up and you head it straight back to me. No! I've seen more power in a wet lettuce. Come on, give it some clout!'

'Volley practice,' he said. 'I'll throw the ball and you kick it. Miss the goalmouth and you'll stink forever! Come on - keep your eye on the ball!'

'Can we open the snack bag now please?' I asked, sucking in a precious gulp of air. 'I'm starving!'

'Just ten more minutes,' Joe replied.

'But you're eating a biscuit!'

'Yes but I'm the boss! Now come on, if you want to get into that team, you have to work for it!'

It was on one of these weekend afternoons that Tony Smith and his friends wandered by.

'What's this?' he snarled, pointing at Joe. 'Some alien training robot or something?'

I wanted to punch his smirking face but something stopped me. 'He's my coach actually,' I snapped as I clenched two sweat soaked fists together. 'You'll have more luck training a chimpanzee, Grandad,' Tony sneered.

At this, Smith and his little gang turned away. Jeering like a pack of hungry hyenas, they sprinted down the hill. Noisy guffaws of laughter faded away as they disappeared into the distance.

'I'm sorry about that,' I said to Joe.

'Don't worry about it,' he replied. 'We'll get our own back on the football pitch.'

'Yeah but he can score goals Joe,' I said.

'And we can work miracles,' Joe replied.

Nine

A few weeks passed. We'd won the semi-final by two goals to one. Tony scored both goals that day and I watched it all from the touchline. Bad weather had postponed the final a few times, so Stanley F.C. hummed with excitement.

I turned up for training, warming up with all the others. 'The final's next weekend everybody,' Barry said. 'And I'll be picking the team later on, straight after training.

Barry glanced over to me. 'Where've you been hiding, Kid?' he shouted out as he jogged past. 'Not seen you in ages!'

'I've not been very well, Barry,' I lied, sprinting towards Joe. Sucking a boiled sweet, he was sat upright in his wheelchair, rather like a powerful Roman Emperor.

'Don't say anything,' he whispered. 'Just let your football do the talking…'

Running back onto the pitch, an incredible energy filled my bones. *It's those invisible batteries stuffed down my socks,* I thought.

I hooked up a football, balancing it on the end of my boot. I kicked it hard, ramming it into the back of the empty net.

'Well done, Malcolm!' Barry shouted. 'Great play Kid!' I couldn't believe it. Every 'rocket' shot was on target. I scored more goals than anybody.

Dribbling like a smooth snake, I curled the ball around Tony Smith's feet. I struck the ball low but hard. A second later, it crashed into the back of the net.

'What on earth have you been eating?' Barry asked. 'Carry on like this and you'll definitely be in the team kid; No doubt about it!'

All the time I was glancing up at Joe. 'Well done Malcolm!' he yelled, clapping like a happy sea lion.

A little later, I was at Joe's house again, playing cards for money. He'd always have the biggest mountain of bronze and silver coins stacked in front of him. Perhaps he cheated.

Carefully, I chose my moment. 'I've been picked for the final, Joe,' I said, my lips grinning wide. 'And Barry said I'm striker, up front with Tony.'

A wide, wrinkly smirk stuck to his lips. Soothing, cooling tears filled his eyes, brightly burning with pride. He bounced up in his armchair, tossing his cards up into the air.

'I always knew you'd do it, Sparrowlegs,' he exclaimed. 'Come here.'

I leaned over Joe and he hugged into me hard, squeezing my arms tight. 'Well done Malcolm, good show!'

'I couldn't have done it without you though,' I replied. 'And what's Sparrowlegs?'

'It's a long story,' Joe replied. 'Anyway, you did all the hard work, not me. If you want something, you've got to work for it, remember!'

Bending down, Joe fished up a few playing cards. For a moment, he fell silent. His eyes glazed over. He lowered his head, tapping his forehead with his chunky fingertips.

Panting, he sucked in deep breaths of air, filling up his lungs. His stomach rose up and down. Blood rushed to his face, changing his colour in an instant.

'What's wrong, Joe?' I asked, clasping his hand.

'Just a little pain in my chest,' he mumbled. 'I suppose I'm just getting old Malcolm. Happens to all of us, eventually.'

Ten

Gulping a mouthful of warm tea, Joe settled down. His breathing was shallow and even. He shuffled around on his chair, resting his back on a cushion. Then he changed the subject.

'Now in the old days, our coach was called Juan Lopez. He'd have us kicking at that white spot on the wall for hours on end, you know. Even in the dark and we had to hit that spot ten times on the run, not five!'

'So who did you play for when you were younger?' I asked. Not answering my question, he stared at me with his old, narrowing eyes.

Pointing to a large wall cupboard, he sat back, stroking his stubbly chin. Charlotte's put all me football stuff in there,' he said. 'But I've lost the flaming key, haven't I?'

'Did you play football a lot then?'

'I was exactly like you, Malcolm. Raw talent I had. I just needed somebody to help me along the way. That's all.'

'Who helped you then?'

'My dad,' he said. 'He didn't work on a Sunday in those days. He'd take me to the big park in Montevideo every single week.'

Joe's eyes clouded over with thick, silvery tears. I could see that he was back in that park, playing with his dad. 'He was killed in a factory accident,' he said, dabbing his eyes with a damp tissue.

'He just went to the yard one day and that was that. We never saw him again. Got caught up in a gas explosion, somebody said. And Mum was never the same after that, never. She died a few years later you know, of a broken heart I think.'

Dropping his head, the pain of yesterday rose up through Joe's frozen bones. Once more he dabbed his eyes with his tissue, shaking his head. I rubbed his arms hard, warming his body up.

'How old were you when he died, Joe?'

'Nine years old,' Joe replied. 'Far too young to have no daddy, if you ask me.'

A rush of cold raced through my spine. My body twitched and shivered. 'I was only nine years old when my dad died, Joe, remember?' I announced.

We both looked at each other, absorbing each other's pain. Young and smooth, old and wrinkled eyes locked together. 'I know what you're feeling, Malcolm,' Joe whimpered.

Two lonely tears rolled down his rough skin, like raindrops clinging to drainpipes. 'Anyway, come over here,' he said.

Hugging into me, he whispered gentle, soothing words into my ear. 'We're like peas in a pod you and me,' he said. 'Peas in a pod!'

'Nobody knows what it's like,' he continued. 'People say they understand but they don't. I still see Dad's face even now, every day. I hear his voice in my dreams too, Malcolm. And I'm almost eighty! I know he's watching me and I can even feel him next to me sometimes.'

'I know exactly what you mean, Joe,' I said, trickling tears trying to escape. 'And my dad's watching me as well!'

Joe sat up. Shaking a long, bony finger, he gazed at me, speaking softly in a calm tone. 'And our dads want you to score in that cup final of yours, don't they?' he said. 'And so do I for that matter and Charlotte of course and your mum!'

'Well I hope I do score, Joe,' I said. 'For everybody.'

'Hey, never mind 'hope so'!' Joe chuckled. 'You're going to score three goals – a hat trick! And I suppose you're going to need those football boots you're always going on about, aren't you?'

Before I could answer, Joe dragged out a small cardboard shoebox. It was sitting by the side of his chair, hiding in a Boydells brown paper bag, covered up with a pile of old newspapers. A wry smile stretched across his face as he handed it to me.

'Something you wanted, Sparrowlegs!' he said. 'I hope they fit!'

'Sparrowlegs?' I asked.

'It's just that it's like looking at me all those years ago,' he replied. 'And that was my old nickname. That's what the crowd used to chant, anyway!'

'What crowd?'

'Oh never mind about me, just open the box!'

Feeling my heart heat up to a warm glow, I smiled. 'Well Sparrowlegs it is then!' I exclaimed, kneeling down on Joe's warm, flattened rug.

Opening the box with shaking fingers, my eyes burned like two hot sparklers on bonfire night. Two panther black, 'Goal hunger' football boots stared out at me, smothered in soft, silver tissue. For a few seconds, I couldn't move.

'You're allowed to take them out,' Joe said. 'They won't bite you!'

Picking one up, I stroked the soft, black material. I pulled the thick, silver laces. Squeezing the boot gently, a strong smell of smooth, polished leather puffed up into my nostrils.

I stared at the six, silver 'screw-in' studs, running my fingertips over them. I couldn't believe what I was holding. I was expecting to wake up with a sudden jolt, ending my heavenly dream.

'They're beautiful Joe,' I said. 'Just beautiful.'

'Your mum went halves with me Malcolm. Saved up for weeks we did! Even Charlotte helped as well and the lady at Boydells knocked a fiver off for you. Said she was fed up of you staring at them in her window on your way home from school!'

'I still can't believe they're mine,' I said, still caressing the boots' soft leather. 'And I'll definitely score that hat-trick now, Joe!'

'Well if you don't score a hat trick in this cup final of yours, I'll take them back to Boydells. And that's a promise!'

I looked up at Joe's face, staring deep into his old, sunken eyes. 'I *will* score a hat-trick on Saturday,' I said. 'And I'll score it for our dads, Joe. And our mums of course and

Charlotte. But most of all, I'll score it for you Joe. For all that you've done for me. And that's a promise too!'

Eleven

Saturday soon arrived. A large crowd gathered for the final, Stanley F.C. versus Harrington Hawks F.C. Both teams 'Under eleven'.

Mum and Charlotte stood together with Joe, one on either side of his wheelchair. Even Graham was there, munching on a huge ham roll. He was more than happy to give Mum a rare Saturday morning off and wanted to watch himself.

'Malcolm, you're striker!' Barry cried as we warmed up. 'Play up front opposite Tony, like I said in training.'

'Cool boots Malcolm,' Tony shouted, his shoulder length blonde hair blowing in the breeze. 'Anyway, are you under some sort of magic spell or something? You've well improved mate!'

A hot spring of happiness leapt up inside me, warming my bones. 'I've just got a brilliant coach Tony, that's all,' I replied. 'He's over there. The one in the wheelchair. I think you've met him before haven't you?'

He didn't have time to reply. A football swooped down low and I dribbled it along, belting it into the back of the net.

Running towards the goalposts, I couldn't stop laughing to myself. I was a stray dog who'd just found the biggest, juiciest bone in the world! A cloud of happiness exploded around me, its silvery stars surrounding me like fairy dust.

Soon, the whistle blew and we kicked off. The ball floated high above my head. It bounced in front of me, sending the remains of a puddle high up into the cold air. I lunged for the ball but just missed and it landed at the feet of a Hawk.

Darting up the field, the Hawk looked up. A short pass did the trick. Another Hawk, a small, thin boy wearing glasses, banged it with incredible strength. It landed at the feet of another Hawk who struck it low, first time.

Our goalkeeper, George, had no chance. He flung his long body across the goals but the ball screeched past him at blistering speed. Not a good start at all.

An army of blue football shirts piled on top of the jubilant goal scorer. 'Don't worry, lads!' Tony yelled, pacing up the touchline. 'Plenty of time left! Just keep your heads up!'

Not long after, disaster struck. The ball trickled towards our goals. George, surrounded by two Hawks, dived, pushing the ball out for a corner ball.

Seconds later, the ball zoomed over my head. Then he appeared out of nowhere, as if he'd been conjured up by a sorcerer.

A tall, skinny Hawk, who towered over us like a thin, blue skyscraper. No wonder they called him 'Scraper'. His head punched into the ball hard. It almost burst as it crashed into the goal's netting.

We had a couple of chances and a few narrow escapes. Half time arrived. The referee blew his shrill whistle. The Hawks' crowd cheered, surrounding their players as they skipped off the pitch.

I glanced across to the wooden scoreboard. 'Harrington Hawks 2, Stanley Village 0' stared out at me, taunting and threatening me. Puffing out long, deflated blows, I glared at my mud-encrusted boots.

'Come on!' I screamed, kicking a large clump of soil up into the air. 'Even Mum's watching!'

'You're all bunching up!' Barry bawled at half time. He screwed up his fat face, staring at us like a wild, uncontrollable beast.

'You're not keeping your shape! You're not staying in position. You need to make space. Mark your man and pass the ball for heaven's sake! Otherwise it's all over!'

I dashed towards Joe for a quick drink.

'Sorry Joe,' I said. 'I think I should have stayed at home. Nothing's going right!'

'Don't worry, love,' Mum said, ruffling up my hair. 'Just go out there and try your best!'

'But nothing's going right Mum!'

'That happens sometimes,' Joe calmly said. 'But listen Malcolm. It's not over yet is it? And remember what I've told you. Be hungry! Imagine those invisible batteries! Fight for the ball. Look for those gaps. Read ahead of the game…and those goals will come. It's as simple as that Sparrowlegs!'

I was just about to reply when the referee's piercing whistle blew. Time for the second half.

'You can win this one, lads!' Barry yelled. 'Weave your magic Tony! And Malcolm, show us all what you can do…just like in training! Let your boots do the talking!'

I will Barry, I thought, taking up position ready for the kick-off. *I'll show you all and I mean it!*

The referee's whistle blew. Minutes later, chasing after the ball, I hooked it up with my right boot. I sprinted as fast as I could, imagining those batteries stuffed down my socks.

I passed a smooth, straight ball to Tony's tired but dancing feet. He weaved his way around two players, sending one of them tumbling to the floor.

I darted up the field towards the goalmouth. Tony tapped the ball back, sending a Hawk the wrong way. Now close to the box, I dribbled around two strong defenders.

Glancing up, I found my place, striking the ball hard. The hot, magical ball flew through the electric air.

Diving, the Hawks' goalkeeper stretched his elastic arms wide. But my well-placed shot was out of his reach. The ball plunged into the back of the net.

Instantly, a mountain of red shirts piled on top of me. They grabbed and pulled me, squeezing and rubbing my head.

'Brilliant Malcolm!' Barry yelled, striding up the touchline. 'Just one more now, son!'

Grinning, I looked over to Joe and punched the air with my fist. He was almost dancing in his wheelchair, waving a red and white Stanley F.C. scarf high over his head.

'Come on Sparrowlegs!' he screamed, throwing his cloth cap into the air.

Soon, I was at it again. I spotted a gap and sprinted through it. One or two Hawks tried to steal the ball away from me. But it seemed to be super-glued to my 'Goal hunger' football boots.

Seconds later, I'd penetrated the Hawks' defence and was in the box. Shooting with all my strength, the ball powered towards the goalmouth but plunged into the crossbar.

But Lady luck was on my side. The ball ricocheted off the woodwork and bounced back towards me. It landed directly in front of my right foot. I lunged at it before it had a chance to land.

My powerful volley flew into the goals like a heat seeking missile. The goalkeeper's fingers touched it but the hot football almost scorched his gloves. The crowd exploded, cheering like crazy. People jumped up and down, splashing watery mud in different directions.

Joe's wheelchair nearly tipped up as he sprung up in his seat. Players chased after me, climbing onto my shoulders one by one.

'Unbelievable!' screamed Tony, patting me on the back. He dropped his jaw wide open, stretching his bright blue eyes wide.

'Three minutes left!' Barry screamed, rapidly banging his hands together. 'We can finish them off now lads. We don't want penalties!'

I waved to Mum and she waved back. Joe and Charlotte waved too, launching huge grins. My heart warmed up and a gentle glow heated my bones. It made a huge difference to have people supporting me, especially Mum, of course.

'Two minutes left!' Barry's loud, deep voice cried out again. 'One minute now, that's all. Come on, lads!'

Twelve

I didn't hear it at first. It was a sort of whisper. Dad's voice it was, rattling around inside my head. He seemed to be calling me from some strange, heavenly place. 'You can do it, Son, you really can!'

Then it was Joe, taunting me with that irritating, favourite saying of his: 'If you want something Malcolm, you've got to work for it, remember!'

As soon as the ball crossed my path, it happened. I scooped it up with my left foot.

Tapping it to my right foot, I juggled with it, like a cat playing with a mouse. Incredible power, like a thousand motorcycle engines revving up at the same time, filled my feet.

I was coated in pure magic. My boots glowed white hot. My heart pumped electric energy into my aching muscles. My whole body vibrated, in tune with the wind.

Quickly, I weaved my way through two Hawk defenders, sending them the wrong way. One fell to the ground and looked at the referee, who fortunately, didn't even react.

Sticking to my feet, the ball seemed to be sewn onto my boots. Scraper stood in my way, like a tall, thin wall of concrete. I swerved my body, keeping the ball close. Snarling, he was sent off balance, crashing into the torn, muddy grass.

Another Hawk shot towards me. He tackled me well but I managed to keep hold of the precious ball. For a second, I was back in Joe's back yard. I saw that white spot on the wall, right in front of my eyes, in the top corner of the goalmouth.

It was a simple, right-footed 'chip' shot. I sent it floating through the air like a skylark on a spring morning. It drifted over the goalkeeper, gently dropping into the back of the net.

Funnily enough, I don't remember a lot of what happened next. I suppose I was in some sort of shock. The Red parts of the crowd jumped for joy towards the sky, landing on invisible springs.

Waving their scarves, they tossed caps and hats high up into the sky. Other Reds sprung up and down, punching the air with closed fists as they hugged each other in warm circles.

Over and over the crowd chanted and chanted. 'Magic Malcolm! Magic Malcolm!'

I stretched my neck up high. I wanted to give Joe a big wave but I couldn't see him. The crowd had gushed forwards. People pushed and shoved, surrounding me.

I did see Barry though. He was bouncing up and down on some sort of invisible trampoline. Water was gushing from his red, plastic bottle, spilling out all over the grass. Hurriedly, I rushed towards my teammates.

A long minute later, we finally kicked off once more. And just a few kicks later, it finally pierced my eardrums. Punching a hole into the Hawks' heavy hearts, it was the final whistle.

Smothered by players, I was soon high up on everybody's shoulders. They paraded me around like some sort of famous superstar.

'Fantastic hat-trick!' beamed Tony, looking up at me. 'You're magic Son!' Barry yelled, patting my back hard. 'Pure magic!'

I was loving it, lapping it all up like a famous footballer with both hands firmly planted on the F.A. cup.

Desperate to see Joe's face, I peered at countless people in the thick crowd. Like a barn owl, I twisted my head around, scanning every face.

And that's when I saw him. He wasn't sitting in his wheelchair any more. Joe was lying on the floor. He was flat out on the grass, his body not moving at all.

'Joe!' I cried out, my eyeballs sticking out like golf balls.

Leaning over him, Mum and Charlotte seemed to be massaging his chest. I shook off my admirers, sprinting over at great speed.

'Call an ambulance!' I heard a voice scream out. I shut off all sounds from my ears. Staring and unable to move, my whole world fell into a cold, empty silence.

Thirteen

Pacing up and down a long, cold corridor, my legs trembled. Mum was at my side, holding my hand. Eventually, we found Joe's little room. Charlotte was already there, sitting on a small plastic chair beside Joe's bed.

She couldn't peel her eyes away from her beloved Uncle. All sorts of tubes and wires hung from his frail body. 'Is Joe going to be alright?' Mum asked, pulling up a chair.

'The specialist said he's had a mild heart attack,' Charlotte answered, wiping tears from her eyes. 'They said he's too old,' she sobbed. 'He's not got the strength you see. He's probably never going to wake up.'

Spluttering, an enormous spring of tears burst out onto her silky tissue. 'Come on, Charlotte,' Mum soothed. 'You look exhausted. Let's go and get a cup of tea from the machine.

Malcolm'll keep an eye on Joe, won't you, love?'

I nodded, staring at Joe's grey, pitted face. A pearly white duvet covered his body. As raspy breaths whistled from his dry mouth, his chest rose up and down. 'You're not giving up on us just yet,' I whispered.

I smiled, forcing back an icy block of melting tears. There was no response. Joe was just lying there. The sound of his heavy breathing cut into the sad, silent, atmosphere. 'Anyway, you're not going anywhere before I've shown you this!' I exclaimed.

Slowly, I lifted my winner's medal over my head. As the spotlights hit it, it shone like the evening star twinkling at dusk. It was pure gold, with a deep engraving of a footballer in the middle. Hanging from its red, silky ribbon, it almost hypnotised me.

A winner's medal for playing football and it was all mine! I still couldn't believe it. I clutched its warm metal in my hand. I ran my fingers up and down the ribbon. But I knew one thing – I had to let it go.

I know I shouldn't have, but I gently lifted Joe's head up. Placing the ribbon over his head, I rested my medal upon his heart. Tears poured out of my red, itching eyes. 'This belongs to you Joe,' I whimpered. 'I didn't win it, you did.'

At this, a rare, magical moment appeared before my eyes. A rare experience, like a shooting star greeting you as it streams across the night sky.

Joe's weak voice sparked into life. He didn't open his eyes. He just spoke to me, slowly, softly, just loud enough for me to hear.

'You're a brilliant footballer Sparrowlegs,' he whispered. 'What a hat-trick!'

'I couldn't have done it without you, though,' I replied, grasping his warm hand.

A gentle smirk appeared on his lips. At last he pulled his big eyes open. They flickered as he got used to the ward's warm, bright lights.

'Thanks for the medal, Malcolm,' he said, his voice soft but stronger. He bent his head a little, staring into my eyes. 'Looks lovely it does. Anyway, I'll do you a swap as soon as we get home because, well, what I've not told you is, well…'

At this point, Joe started spluttering. Struggling for breath, his bony fingers gripped my hand tight. His face changed colour. It was a grey, a dark and misty, thunderstorm grey. His body rattled on the bed. Loud beeping noises escaped from computer monitors, piercing my heavy heart.

'Joe!' I screamed as a small army of doctors and nurses rushed into the room.

'Stand clear!' a tall, dark doctor shouted out.

I couldn't bear it any longer.

Weeping wildly, I let go of Joe's limp hand. I turned upon my heels. I couldn't watch any more. Sprinting out of the room, I dashed down the corridor, barging straight into Mum and Charlotte.

Screaming, Charlotte dashed towards Joe's room. Her shoes clattered on the smooth, polished floor like a horse's hooves. I was left with Mum, sobbing into her soft, silky skirt.

Fourteen

'You daft dope!' Joe chuckled from his rocking chair a week or two later. 'I'm not leaving you. Well not just yet anyway!'

A wide, satisfying smile stretched across my face. My medal was still hanging around Joe's neck. He hadn't yet taken it off.

'What happened?' I asked, bouncing down on the sofa.

'The old heart's playing up again, that's all,' he said. 'Everything's wearing out isn't it?'

'I thought you…'

'I know what you thought, Malcolm,' he smiled. 'Anyway, I couldn't go without giving you this, could I?'

He turned towards a small, circular table and picked up an old, battered shoebox. His hands trembled a little as he opened the lid.

Slowly, Joe pulled out another box, a little one, covered in blue velvet.

'What is it?' I asked as he placed it into my hands.

'Open it up and see,' Joe said, sitting upright.

Raising my eyelids, I pulled open the lid, which sprung upright. My beating heart almost burst as a little piece of treasure grabbed my attention.

It was a small, hexagonal football medal, with a raised border. An engraved lady was standing on a platform in the middle, her long arms outstretched, rather like an important angel.

It was all cast in solid, brushed gold. Engraved at the top, in small capital letters, was 'FIFA'.

'Wow, who did this belong to?' I asked, unable to peel my eyes away.

'You can take it out if you want to,' Joe whispered. 'Have a good look at it. Go on!'

He didn't turn his gentle gaze away from me. He just stared at me, like a loving Father watching his son opening up a present on Christmas morning.

Carefully, I pulled the medal from its velvety home. I held it high, holding it by its thin, fragile clasp. Crashing into it, a thick, golden light dazzled my eyes. The engraved footballer seemed to come to life in my hands, belting the ball high.

'Notice anything?' Joe asked, with that familiar, cheeky grin of his. I was about to say no when I turned the medal over. The incredible words 'World cup winners – Uruguay' shot into my widening eyes, along with Juan Schiaffino.

'What the,' I gasped, gazing at the medal as it rested in my soft palm.

'I told you I wasn't bad, didn't I?' he chuckled.

'Is it really yours, Joe?' I asked, as my stretching eyes almost burst open.

'Of course it is, you daft dope!' Joe replied, ruffling up my hair. 'Anyway, it's yours,' he said. 'A little present for working so hard for me.'

'I can't take this Joe,' I said, shaking my head. 'I mean, well, it belongs to you and your family really, doesn't it?'

'Maria and I couldn't have any children Malcolm,' Joe said. 'Nearly drove us insane it did.'

Pausing, Joe's eyes flooded with a wash of clear, lubricating tears. I stared deep into them, delving into his painful past. Two deep, dark tunnels stared out at me, haunted by the raw pain of long, long ago.

'Years ago, I'd have given that medal away for the chance of a baby,' he added. 'Impossible it was in those days. So that's why I'm giving it to you, Malcolm. You've been my little boy, you see. The boy I could never, ever have.'

'I can't take it Joe,' I said. 'I just can't, it's yours!'

Lovingly, he gazed at me with wide, drooping eyes. 'If you don't take it, I'll take my football boots back!' he chuckled.

A wry smile appeared on his face. 'Just make sure you never sell it, even when times are hard,' he said. He clasped his bony hands around my medal, still hanging around his neck.

'You keep that one and I'll keep this one,' he said, throwing out another cheeky grin. 'A fair swap I'd say!'

Fifteen

The room fell into silence as we both stared at our precious, golden treasures.

'I was doing nothing before I met you Malcolm,' he said. 'I was just sitting there, watching the box all day. But for the first time in my life, I felt like somebody's dad. And that's all down to you Malcolm. All down to you!'

Stretching those long, baggy wrinkles, his mouth broke out into an enormous smile. Joe bowed his head, running his hands over those few remaining strands of silver hair.

Two gentle tears slipped out of his narrow eyes as he locked his loving gaze onto me. He dabbed his eyes with a soft tissue, chuckling once more. 'I'm a stupid old fool, aren't I?' he chuckled, rolling his eyes around.

'No you're not,' I shouted out, playfully pointing a finger at him. 'You're just a great big softie, that's all!'

'When I'm gone, will you promise me something? Joe asked.

'Hey, you've got a long time to go yet,' I replied.

'I hope so, Malcolm,' Joe added, shrugging his shoulders. 'But who knows eh? I've had a good innings as they say!'

'Well I think you've got years left in you, so don't start saying anything daft!'

'Anyway Malcolm,' Joe said, staring into my eyes. 'Promise me that you'll always play your football. Teach your children football too if they want to play. But most of all, promise me this Malcolm. Whenever you look at my medal, whenever you hold it, touch it and feel it, remember me. Good old Joe!'

'Of course I will,' I announced, holding back two escaping tears. I skipped over to Joe and bounced upon his bony knee. Closing my eyes, I hugged into him, whispering into his hairy ear. 'I'll never forget you, Dad.'

We almost squeezed the life out of each other. Love filled our bones, welding us together as one. 'Friends forever, Dad,' I whispered softly.

'Hey, nobody can ever replace your real dad, Malcolm,' Joe sniffed. 'Remember that, it's important.'

'Well I'll call you Grandad then' I beamed. 'And well, I, I, I, because, well, I love you, that's why!'

'Well I love you too, Malcolm,' Joe spluttered. 'I love you too.' Old tears and young tears mingled, forming a fountain of pure love.

Wiping my eyes, I glanced over Joe's shoulder. A long, cold shiver wriggled up my spine. My head wouldn't move, hypnotised by the unfolding scene in front of me. My wispy breathing ceased. I drew in a sharp, shocked breath of air, my body frozen to the spot.

Hopping across an old chest of drawers, a little robin stopped. His head twitched from side to side. His shining, brown eyes peered at me for an age, burning into my spirit.

A strong, golden light surrounded him. Tiny, silver stars spun around his little brown, body, bathed in that strange but peaceful light.

For several seconds, he just stayed there, dancing across the smooth, mahogany surface. His tiny eyes locked onto me, gazing into me. Then he flapped his fragile wings and lifted up into the air, accompanied by his starry, golden light.

His wings carried him to the edge of an open window. Turning his head, he stared at me for one, final time, proudly displaying his red breast. And then, he was gone.

'I love you, Dad,' I whispered as my mouth widened into a gentle smile. 'I love you so much. And I'll never forget you.'

'Right,' Joe announced, pulling away from me. 'Let's open up my football cupboard. And no more crying, I'm fed up of it!'

'It's you who always starts it!' I said, shaking a finger at him. 'Anyway, what sort of stuff's in there?'

'It's a secret until you open it,' Joe replied. 'Just all my footy stuff from my playing day, that's all; Cups, medals, caps, a few old shirts, you'll know the sort of stuff.'

He dangled a small brass key on a string in front of me. 'I found the key!' he exclaimed. 'Stuck to the bottom of my slippers!'

'Trust you,' I chuckled, taking it from his grasp. I stared at the key resting in my palm.

Then I looked at the lock, high up on the tall cupboard. 'How on earth am I going to reach up there?' I asked.

'You'll have to stand on a chair,' Joe replied, shaking his head. 'Because if you want something, you've got to work for it. Remember that, Sparrowlegs!'

Stanley Village 3

Harrington Hawks 2

Juan Schiaffino's

1950 World cup winner's medal

Juan Alberto Schiaffino

(1925 – 2002)

On July 16th 1950, the day of the World cup final, Rio newspaper, 'O Mundo' carried this headline: **'THESE ARE THE WORLD CHAMPIONS!'** alongside a picture of the Brazilian football team. An estimated 200,000 fans streamed into the giant concrete arena in anticipation of Brazil's coronation as footballing 'Champions of the world'.

Brazil's legendary 'Maracana' stadium
(Rio de Janiero)

Alcides Ghiggia scores the winning goal!

Opponents Uruguay, just clinching victory over Sweden in their previous game, were seen as the underdogs, easy prey for Brazil's fantastic team. This seemed to be coming true when Friaca put Brazil ahead early in the second half.

Juan Alberto Schiaffino equalised, but Brazil remained on course for the trophy until Uruguay winger Alcides Ghiggia surprised Brazil's goalkeeper Barbosa with a low shot in the 79th minute that stunned the giant stadium into a cold, icy silence.

Uruguay, not Brazil, were crowned world champions and the host nation sank into mourning. Barbosa became an instant scapegoat and played for his country only once more.

Nelson Rodrigues, a Brazilian playwright, called the defeat 'A national catastrophe!'

In response, a competition was launched by Rio newspaper 'Correio da Manha' to redesign the uninspiring white strip that Brazil's players had worn in the final.

The winning entry, submitted by a young, 19-year-old illustrator called Aldyr Garcia Schlee, combined the yellow, green and blue of the Brazilian flag and is worn by Brazil's footballers to this day.

Uruguay's victorious team

Juan Schiaffino is still regarded as the finest player to emerge from Uruguay. He was an inside forward with a tremendous range of passing, speed, vision and a very fierce shot!

He was instrumental in Uruguay's victory in the 1950 World cup, ending the tournament as the second highest goalscorer, with 5 goals. He even scored the equaliser in the final and the icing on the cake was setting up the winning goal for Ghiggia, with only 11 minutes of the match remaining.

What a legendary footballer!

Uruguay 2

Brazil 1

Sometimes, dreams really do come true…

Lightning Source UK Ltd.
Milton Keynes UK
UKHW04f1949180918
329129UK00001B/267/P